CHILLERS

CHILLERS
Clive and the Missing Finger

Sarah Garland

PUFFIN BOOKS

PUFFIN BOOKS

Published by the Penguin Group
Penguin Books Ltd, 27 Wrights Lane, London W8 5TZ, England
Penguin Putnam Inc., 375 Hudson Street, New York,
New York 10014, USA
Penguin Books Australia Ltd, Ringwood, Victoria, Australia
Penguin Books Canada Ltd, 10 Alcorn Avenue, Toronto, Ontario,
Canada M4V 3B2
Penguin Books (NZ) Ltd, Private Bag 102902, NSMC,
Auckland, New Zealand

Penguin Books Ltd, Registered Offices: Harmondsworth,
Middlesex, England

First published by A & C Black (Publishers) Ltd 1994
Published in Puffin Books 1995
10 9 8 7

Chapter One

Mad Dogs

I put my eye to the crack in the fence and my hair stood on end! A horde of slavering dogs were hurling themselves at me, shrieking, snarling, hitting the planks so they rocked! Spit came flying right through the crack!

This was the first time I had set foot in my new back garden. What a welcome!

My heart was thudding, but I turned round slowly to walk indoors. I wasn't going to let *them* see I was frightened.

"What's going on?" shouted Dad, jumping from the back door down on to the grass.

The dogs were howling now, all together, like coyotes in a cowboy film, or wolves creeping closer to some lonely trapper by a campfire in the wild North.

"Don't you go disturbing them dogs!" shouted someone angrily from behind the fence.

Dad and I turned towards the voice.

"That'll be our neighbour, Mr Tibbald," said Dad wryly.

There was a crash, and a scraping, clanking noise. Someone was dragging something to the fence, climbing on to it and breathing heavily. Two hands appeared, white knuckled, then a face reared up, red and twisted with rage.

IF YOU GOES NEAR THEM DOGS YOU'LL GET WHAT YOU DESERVES!

I only saw him for a moment or two, but for some reason every line on his twitching face, every thin carrotty hair on his scalp, was stamped on my mind for ever. It was shocking seeing him like that, suddenly, against the sky.

6

He lifted a fist
and shook it at us, then
spread his calloused fingers wide.
My breath caught. His right index
finger was missing. There was just an
angry red stump.

"Yes young fellow. I sees you gasp. T'was
Rex, the big mastiff, he mistook it for a
lump of meat. Let that be a lesson to . . ."

Crumbs!

. . . Another crash and our neighbour swayed wildly and disappeared as suddenly as he had come. We heard shuffling steps, barking and curses.

Dad put his arm round me as we walked back up the garden.

"I can see now why we got this place so cheaply," he said thoughtfully.

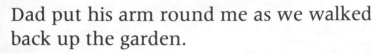

Chapter Two

Dad Tries to be Cheerful

Dad was cheery at breakfast, he was trying really hard. Since he had been made redundant our lives had changed a lot.

"I'll get some ear-plugs today," he said. "Then it'll be easier to sleep through the barking."

"That's right. Think positive," said Dorrie, my big sister.

Dad gave Dorrie a funny look.

"What have you gone and done to yourself?" he said.

Dorrie frowned. She'd put on lipstick and there were peculiar orange patches down her cheek bones and black bits round her eyes. She didn't look nice at all.

"You go straight upstairs and wash that off," said Dad in a strangled voice.

"Dad . . ." wailed Dorrie, "I'm starting at sixth form *college*, not *school*."

I'm nearly SEVENTEEN!

I left them at it
and went upstairs to put on
my new uniform.

It was terrible. Dad had bought trousers
about three sizes too big. I looked at
myself in the mirror on the landing as
the trousers slithered slowly down to
my knees.

I hauled them up
and ran down
the stairs.

Ten minutes later
Dorrie had left, her
face scrubbed pink
and her brow like
thunder.

Dad was still sewing up my trouser
bottoms. He looked sadly at his enormous
stitches.

"Good luck with the
book, Dad," I said as
I left for the bus.

I had great hopes
for the book.
Dad had decided to
use some of his
redundancy money
for us to live on
while he tried to
write a mystery thriller.

I tried to think of Dad as
a best selling author so
I wouldn't have to think
about my first day at a
new school.

I was the only one at the bus stop,
and my stomach knotted up tight
while I waited. When I got on the bus
everybody stopped talking and had a good
look at me.

I didn't look at them.
They were just a blur.
I looked out of the
window all the
way to the school.

Well, after all, it was like most schools.
Assembly, and the head talking away
about doing our best, and us singing a
hymn, and the piano out of tune.
I'd get through it all right.

Mrs Suffolk, our class teacher, looked odd
but she was friendly. She kept cages
of mice in the classroom, and a snake,
and jars of innards that smelt peculiar,
and a microscope.

She said I could be in charge of the mice, so I fed them in the lunch-hour.

At the end of the day I walked home from the bus stop feeling completely worn out.

Dad opened the door and hugged me tight. I looked under his arm into the kitchen and was amazed.

Dorrie was there already, guzzling away at a mountainous tea. Sausage-rolls, bacon and egg pie, sandwiches, a fruit cake, a trifle loaded with cherries. I couldn't believe my eyes.

"Did you *buy* all this, Dad?"

"I made it," said Dad proudly. "I found this cookery book . . ."

WOW!

"Dad," said Dorrie severely (though her mouth was full of pastry crumbs which blew out in little gusts). "I thought you were supposed to be *writing* a book, not *reading* one."

Dad turned away and lit the gas under the kettle.

"It's not that easy, Dorrie. You've got to have some inspiration, you know, to write a mystery thriller. It'll come, I know it will."

"Of course it will, Dad."

Chapter Three

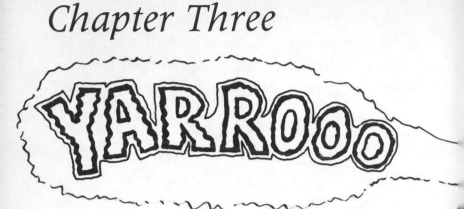

That night the dogs next door howled worse than ever. Rain blew in great gusts against my window and even my earplugs couldn't shut out the noise.

By midnight the dogs were really wild. We watched them from my bedroom window as they leaped at the fence, yowling and gnashing their teeth.

Next morning, Dad went down and knocked hard and long on Mr Tibbald's door, but there was no answer.

"I'll have to ring the police," he said.

"Let me stay away from school and watch," I begged.

"Of course not, Clive. Not on your second day."

So I didn't find out what had happened until I saw the newspaper hoardings on the way back from school.

LOCAL
RECLUSE
MYSTERY
MAN GOES
MISSING

said one.

said another.

I burst through the door. Dad was stirring something on the stove.

"Tell me Dad, quick!" I cried.

He turned a flushed face towards me. The kitchen was hot and filled with wonderful smells.

"Today I have mastered the art of choux pastry," he said.

Dorrie and I looked at each other across the kitchen table. She raised her eyebrows and shrugged.

21

"THE DOGS, DAD! THE POLICE!"

"Ah yes," said Dad, pouring chocolate sauce over a mound of profiteroles. "That *was* a drama. The police had quite a struggle with the dogs: sedated them, carried them off to the dogs' home, spent all day searching the house for clues. Mmm . . . try this Dorrie. Anyway, they found evidence that old Tibbald had escaped from prison and had been living here secretly for about ten years. Mmm . . . yum . . . not bad. But, for some reason, he ran off last night. Can't say I'm sorry. Have a profiterole, love."

Deeeeelishus!

I said absently, cream spurting out between my teeth.

Mr Tibbald a convict! But why had he suddenly run away? He must have been desperate to have left his dogs. I felt an insatiable curiosity. I began to do my famous Sherlock Holmes impersonation, screwing up my eyes against the pipe smoke and peering through an imaginary magnifying **glass.**

"And the other good news," said Dad, "is that I've got an allotment. I haven't been able to find the ingredients for all my recipes in the shops so I've decided to grow them myself."

"That's good, Dad."

Dorrie sighed and glanced at the typewriter in the corner. There was dust on the cover already, and the pile of paper beside it was untouched.

"This food is going to ruin my figure," she complained, biting into warm, sugary pastry, filled with currants. "What is this, anyway?"

Eccles cake, darling. I've added a touch of chopped mint. Like it?

Mmm... yes!

groaned Dorrie licking her fingers.

Chapter Four

The Diamond Gang

Weeds grew up
around Mr Tibbald's house.

I made a hole under the fence and
began to use the overgrown garden for
games and as my secret place.

I didn't mean to go inside the house, but I
kept fiddling absent-mindedly with the
planks the police had used to board up
the windows. One day a plank came off
in my hand, the next day another slid
sideways, and on the third day my
curiosity became so strong that it seemed
to propel me through the kitchen
window.

Empty tins rolled
from under my feet,
making a shocking noise,
and I stood with my back
against the wall, adjusting
to the gloom and trying not
to breathe in the stink.

The little kitchen was the partner to our
kitchen next door, but instead of our
bright whitewashed room with its
pictures and pots and warm smells, this
was like the lair of a wild animal – no,
worse – an animal wouldn't live like this.
Thick grease and grime spattered the
walls, and rags, newspapers and bones
were heaped in the corners.

A little breeze blew through the gap in the window and stirred the rubbish on the floor. A scrap of newspaper shifted on the mantelpiece and began to drift slowly downwards, until it settled at my feet. I picked it up and held it to the light from the window.

This is what it said:

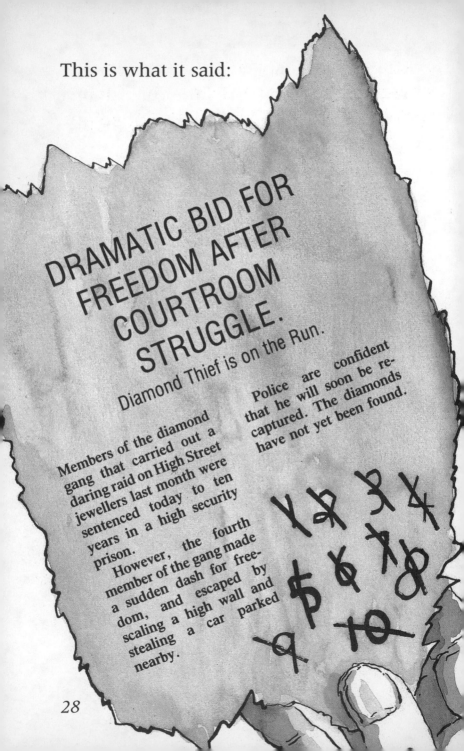

DRAMATIC BID FOR FREEDOM AFTER COURTROOM STRUGGLE.

Diamond Thief is on the Run.

Members of the diamond gang that carried out a daring raid on High Street jewellers last month were sentenced today to ten years in a high security prison.

However, the fourth member of the gang made a sudden dash for freedom, and escaped by scaling a high wall and stealing a car parked nearby.

Police are confident that he will soon be re-captured. The diamonds have not yet been found.

Someone had scrawled marks under the newsprint. Could they be a code? Then I looked at the date. The newspaper was just over ten years old!

I climbed out into the bright sunlight and sat among the weeds to read the cutting again. I didn't need the brain of Sherlock Holmes to work this one out.

Mr Tibbald must be the fourth member of the diamond gang.

The rest of the gang had just been released from prison.

The gang wanted the diamonds.

Mr Tibbald had the diamonds.

The gang wanted revenge.

Mr Tibbald had vanished.

The next day, at school, another piece of the puzzle fell horribly into place.

Chapter Five

After assembly, Mrs Suffolk passed me in the corridor.

"Come and help me, Clive. I've got a surprise for the class today."

"What is it?"

"A secret. Here. It's in this box."

Together we carried it to the classroom.

"It came in the post," said Mrs Suffolk, her eyes sparkling. "No note, nothing. It's an anonymous gift to the school."

The class crowded round. Mrs Suffolk lifted the lid and folded back the tissue paper.

There lay a pile of yellowed bones and, wrapped separately, a skull – a human skull!

"We're going to spend the whole morning putting it together," said Mrs Suffolk. "Here's some wire and a chart of a skeleton for us to copy. I'll show you how."

We each did separate bits. I did the backbones, which were fiddly but not as difficult as the hands and feet. Susan and Godfrey did them. We were all so absorbed and interested we didn't even stop at breaktime.

At last the skeleton hung, complete.

Or almost complete.

"Please, Miss," said Susan. "There are just two little bones I can't find."

This finger's missing!

We looked for the bones everywhere. In the tissue paper, in the box, under the desks.

Those finger bones
were nowhere
to be found.

33

Chapter Six

I Lose my Appetite

I felt very peculiar at lunchtime. My head was spinning. Could it be coincidence? Or was it the most brilliant and bare-faced way to dispose of a body ever thought of?

But how do you get the bones out of a body? Don't you have to boil them?

"Tough pork isn't it? Blimey, I wonder how long they've cooked this for," said Godfrey, beside me.

I choked.

He thumped me on the back.

"What's up, Clive? You look really green! Have a drink of water."

I put my head in my hands. Hadn't I read somewhere that human flesh tastes like pork, only sweeter?

"Godfrey," I croaked. "Do you think this tastes sort of sweet?"

"Um . . . yes . . . I think you're right. Here. It'll go down nicely with some gravy and apple sauce."

I sat up straight.

Pull yourself together, Clive, I said to myself sternly. NOBODY would do a thing like that.

At teatime, I couldn't even look at Dad's steak and kidney pudding.

"Come on, Clive, I need your opinion. Have I been too heavy-handed with the kidneys?" asked Dad.

He'd given up all pretence at writing now. The typewriter had been stowed away in the attic and he spent all day shopping, cooking, or down on the allotment. He was working his way steadily backwards through the cookery book, starting with 'Cakes, Puddings and Savouries' and had reached "Main Dishes'. Next week it would be 'Salads and Starters'.

Dorrie had brought a boyfriend to tea. He was called Zac, had a pony tail and wore leather trousers with studs on them.

Dorrie said to him, "It'll be a relief when we get to salads. This fatty stuff isn't very healthy."

"Oh, I don't know," said Zac, mildly, accepting another steaming plateful.

Dad looked at me anxiously.

"You do look rather peaky, Clive," he said.

The allotments were over the wall at the bottom of the garden. Dad's was at the far end, all neatly dug over and measured out in straight lines.

"Here are the salads," he said, "nearly ready for next week. Not just lettuces, see, but lots of other sorts, and each with its own taste and goodness. Try this peppery one; full of Vitamin C. Now over there, that was old Tibbald's allotment, and I'm thinking I might take it over, then I'd have more land and a shed as well."

I hadn't really been listening until he said the name 'Tibbald'. Then my brain sprang to attention.

Mr Tibbald's allotment was all nettles and brambles, but the hut was in good shape. There could be clues there.

I felt obstinate and cross, like an old bulldog worrying a bone. I was going to solve this mystery once and for all. I decided to come back later, with a torch.

Chapter Seven

BIKERS

Back at the house, Zac was standing beside a huge red motor bike, strapping on his helmet.

Dorrie said, "Just going down the café, Dad, for a coke."

She looked at me.

"Want to come, Clive?"

"Wouldn't mind," I said.

"Would it cheer you up if you had a go on the bike?" she said.

"Yes."

I could see Dad was having a bit of a struggle over that one.

"It's only round
the corner, Dad. He'd
wear a helmet. I'll walk,"
said Dorrie.

"Fine by me," grunted Zac.

So there I was, gripping the pillion
between my knees, helmet on my head
and the road whizzing past just under my
feet. It felt great.

I liked the café. Pinball and fruit-
machines were flashing, there were lots
of mirrors and a juke box, and the door
swung as bikers came and went.

My appetite came back. I had a plate of
chips while Zac and Dorrie talked to their
friends.

This is what I need, I thought, some
distraction to take my mind off Tibbald
and those old bones.

40

And
as that name
came to my mind, I
heard it spoken out loud.

"Calls himself Tibbald," said a thickset
biker at the counter. "Heard of him,
have you?"

I whipped round.

Two other men jostled up behind the biker. They leaned on their elbows and fixed the waitress with glittering eyes.

"Well then," said the waitress, "Haven't you heard? He's the 'Local Recluse'. The 'Mystery Man gone Missing'. Him with the 'Wild Dogs'. It was all in the paper."

"Address?" demanded the thickset man.

"23 Bellevue Terrace. The last house on the left.

They're the ones with the allotments
behind. Now I'll take your orders
if you please."

But the three men turned
with one accord and
vanished through
the swinging
door.

Manners!

So, clever Sherlock, you were completely wrong!

I sat there, my chips going soggy.

The diamond gang hadn't got Mr Tibbald. They hadn't boiled him up and sent his bones to Mrs Suffolk; they were still hunting for him – and hot on the trail.

Mr Tibbald must be hiding out. Where?

Why not in his allotment shed? He could have bought a store of food, and there was a hosepipe tap nearby. He could be waiting until the gang gave up the hunt. Then he would escape with the loot to Australia or South America.

Was I right? I had to find out.

"Can we go home, Dorrie?"

She looked at me.

"Sure, Clive," she said.

Chapter Eight

The Hunt Begins

In the shadows,
outside number 23,
three motor bikes leaned
against the fence.

I left Dorrie and Zac saying goodnight to
each other, and slipped round the back of the
house to collect a torch from the scullery.

I jumped over the garden wall into the
allotments and ran to the far end.
Dad's rows of salads gleamed palely
in the dusk.

I pushed at the door of Mr Tibbald's
allotment shed. Locked,
of course,

I tried the little window. It had no glass, only a thin bit of plastic. I cut the plastic with my Swiss army knife and wriggled through.

I stood listening. There was no sound, but the smell was unmistakable, the same awful, musky stink as in Mr Tibbald's house.

I switched on the torch and swung the
beam round the hut. It lit up a pile of
rags and old coats in the corner.

What the heck was I doing here?

My heart was beating,
thumping, in my
throat; the noise
it made seemed
very loud.

An arm
was stretched
out from under
the rags. A hand, with
curled fingers. Three fingers.
And one red, angry stump. Could
those men have got here before me?
Was I too late? Was Mr Tibbald dead?

With a sudden, violent movement the hand jerked upwards. Then Mr Tibbald was on his feet, a stick in his hand.

"Keep away, boys!" he gasped, hoarsely.

"It's me, Mr Tibbald. Clive. From next door."

Mr Tibbald swore violently.

"The diamond gang, Mr Tibbald, they're after you, they're on their way."

Chapter Nine

I stared out of the window, horror stricken.

On the far side of the allotments, three dim figures were quartering the ground like hounds on a hot scent.

Mr Tibbald was beside me. He was panting with fright.

"We must get out, Mr Tibbald."

"Me diamonds. They're here. Under the floor."

"No time. Come on. Open the door."

Mr Tibbald was shaking so hard, I had to draw back the bolts myself.

"We'll run to the hedge and through to the road," I whispered.

"Can't," whimpered Mr Tibbald.

But I
pulled him
out of the hut,
and together we rushed
at the hedge and forced our
way through, crashing, making
a terrible racket.

Behind us the men set up a sort of baying
shout that scared me so I was icy cold.

We were on the pavement under the
orange lights in the empty road.
Mr Tibbald looked awful.

We ran,

but my . . . legs . . .

didn't . . . seem . . . to be . . .

working . . . properly . . . , like . . .

in . . . a . . . nightmare.

The men were pounding down the hill
behind us, silent now, and intent.

VAROOM

A motor bike. Red.
Turning into the street and
revving towards us up the hill.
Astride it, a figure in black leather.
I half fell off the pavement,
tried to shout – my voice was gone.

It was Zac!

He saw the men, swerved round in a
great skid and we leaped on to the bike,
Mr Tibbald on the pillion, me in front,
jammed on the petrol tank.

"Police station!" I yelled.

Zac raised a thumb.

54

Bits of motor bike
stuck into my thighs,
my knees, my bum. The wind
hurt my ears. I couldn't find anything
to hold on to properly.

But somehow my body found
its balance until it bent so beautifully
with the swoop and glide of the powerful
machine that I felt like a bird, soaring up
the dual carriageway, wheeling round
the curve of the roundabout, and hurtling
at last down the High Street towards the
blue light of the police station.

Chapter Ten

rel Deliverance

I stood on the pavement, the world whirling around me, my ears singing, my eyes stinging.

"Wow Zac! What a ride!"

We stumbled, all three of us,
into the station.

I had to sit down
for a long time,
wrapped up in a rug,
drinking very sweet tea.

A squad of police set off to dig up the diamonds

Mr Tibbald was taken off to the cells.

Dad came, and Dorrie, both as white as sheets.

The police marched
back with a dirty
old box and the
diamond gang
caught red-handed.

Zac made a statement.
I'm making mine
tomorrow.

Then we drove home in a
police car. I suppose
it was quite exciting
with the light flashing
and emergency calls
coming through on the
radio, but after that ride
with Zac it felt rather
ordinary.

When we got home I couldn't face going to bed, so we sat in the kitchen and drank hot milk and I told them the story.

"You know, Dad," I said. "You could write a smashing mystery thriller about some horrible murderer who gives the skeletons of his victims to school science classes."

Dad nibbled a cheese straw.

"Actually," he said, "I've been thinking about giving up writing and opening a café instead. Just a small one to start with. Why don't *you* write it, Clive?"

"All right," I said.

P.S.

It was the last day of term and the last lesson.

We'd nearly finished clearing up when Godfrey said, "Miss, there's a funny rattling noise in the pipe under the sink. Shall I unscrew it and see what it is?"

Mrs Suffolk said, "Yes, do."

Godfrey said, "Oh, it's just some old bones."

Susan said, "They aren't just *any* old bones."

I didn't even need to look.

"I know," I said. "It's THE MISSING FINGER."

Some other Puffin Chillers

CHILLERS

The Day
Matt Sold
Great-grandma

Eleanor Allen
Illustrated by
Jane Cope

It was only an old photograph. Matt thought no
one would even miss it. But he soon begins to
wish he had left it in the attic when his great-
grandma comes back from the dead to haunt
him!

CHILLERS

Jimmy Woods and the Big Bad Wolf

Mick Gowar
Illustrated by
Barry Wilkinson

Jimmy Woods is the worst sort of bully, the sort
that likes hurting people. But there is one thing
he's really scared of and he's about to get the
fright of his life!

CHILLERS

The Real Porky Philips

Mark Haddon

Porky Philips is the story of a boy whom no one
really notices. Even his family can't tell the
difference between him and the mysterious
double who threatens to take his place . . .

Coming soon in Puffin Chillers

CHILLERS

The Blob

Tessa Potter
Illustrated by
Peter Cottrill

The first blob appeared on Graham's book after
second break. It was a rusty red colour and it
looked suspiciously like blood.

Where did the sinister blobs come from? And did
they have something to do with the locked
classroom upstairs, or the strange new
headteacher?

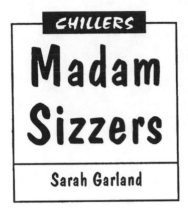

CHILLERS

Madam Sizzers

Sarah Garland

There's something creepy about Madam Sizzers.
Perhaps it's just her sharp red fingernails and her
gleaming scissors. Rachel and Lola try to annoy
her, but then they stumble upon a dark secret...

CHILLERS
Spooked

Philip Wooderson
Illustrated by
Jane Cope

The note said 'Please help me', and with it was a
dusty old photograph of a pale-looking girl. Pete
tried to forget them. Then he saw the face at the
window of the empty house. The same girl's face.
Who was she? Pete had to find out, and that
meant going into the house. Alone.